B★Witched backstage pass

by Kristen Kemp

Your Spellbinding Keepsake Scrapbook

SCHOLASTIC INC.

New York   Toronto   London   Auckland   Sydney   Mexico City   New Delhi   Hong Kong

This unofficial scrapbook is not authorized by or affiliated with B*Witched, their management, or Sony Music Entertainment Inc.

photo credits:

front cover: Ilpo Musto/London Features; **back cover:** Patrick Ford/Redferns/ Retna

interior: p. 3 Joseph Galea; p. 4 Colin Bell/Retna; p. 6 Ilpo Musto/London Features; p. 7 (top) Brigitte Engl/Redferns/Retna; (bottom) John Gladwin/All Action/Retna; p. 8 (top) Jay Blakesberg/Retna; (bottom) David Wardle/Retna; p. 9 Niklas Dahlskog/Famous; p. 10 Sebastiano Pessina/Famous; p. 11 (left) John Gladwin/All Action/Retna; (right) Joseph Galea; p. 12 (top) Wilberto Boogaard Sunshine/Retna; (bottom) David Wardle/Retna; p. 13 Steve Granitz/Retna; p. 14 (bottom) Jill Douglas/Redferns/Retna; p. 15 (top) Brigitte Engl/Redferns/Retna; p. 16 Sebastiano Pessina/Famous; p. 17 (left) John Gladwin/All Action/Retna; (right) Joseph Galea; p. 18 (top) Cameron Bloom/London Features; (bottom) David Wardle/Retna; p. 19 (top) David Wardle/Retna; (bottom) David Wardle/Retna; p. 20 Mark Allan/Globe Photos; p. 21 (bottom) Doug Peters/All Action/Retna; p. 22 Sebastiano Pessina/Famous; p. 23 (left)) Brigitte Engl/Redferns/Retna; (right) Joseph Galea; p. 25 (top) David Wardle/Retna; (bottom) Peter Atchison/Famous; p. 26 Cameron Bloom/London Features; p. 27 (bottom) David Hogan/All Action/Retna; p. 28 Sebastiano Pessina/Famous; p. 29 (left) Steve Granitz/Retna; (right) Joseph Galea; p. 30 (top) Sebastiano Pessina/Famous; (bottom) Duncan Raban/All Action/Retna; p. 31 (top) Brigitte Engl/Redferns/Retna; p. 32 (top) John Gladwin/All Action/Retna; (bottom) Mark Shenley/Retna; p. 33 Joseph Galea; p. 35 Jay Blakesberg/Retna; p. 36 JM Enternational/Redferns/Retna; p. 37 Patrick Ford/Retna; p. 39 (all) Sebastiano Pessina/Famous; p. 40 Patrick Ford/Redferns/Retna; p. 41 Wilberto Boogaard Sunshine/Retna; p. 42 (top) Sebastiano Pessina/Famous; (bottom) Mark Allan/Globe Photos; p. 43 (top) David Fisher/London Features; (bottom) Jen Lowery/London Features; p. 44 Niklas Dahlskog/Famous; p. 45 David Tonge/Retna; p. 46 Colin Bell/Retna; p. 47 Joseph Galea; p. 48 Jay Blakesberg/Retna.

ISBN 0-439-08227-7

Cover Design by Peter Koblish
Interior Design by Jenell Qu

12 11 10 9 8 7 6 5 4 3 2 1   9/9 0 1 2 3 4/0

Printed in the U.S.A.
First Scholastic printing, November 1999

Table of Contents

B★Witched

Chapter 1 B*Witched Is Born!

Why is the world so, well, *bewitched* with B*Witched? That's an easy one! First of all, the kickin' pop group is made up of four super-cool girls — Sinead, Lindsay, Edele, and Keavy — who sing and dance like divas. Second, they have killer attitudes and to-die-for denim duds. Talk about all-around spellbinding! And there's *soooo* much more . . . .

Baby B*Witches

It all started with **Edele and Keavy Lynch.** Way back in the eighties, when they were wee girls, these twins started belting out tunes and making up dances while playing at home in Dublin, Ireland. Unlike other kids who play around with music, these two were singin' *constantly.* "No question about it," Edele says, "we always knew we wanted to be in a band together." Then it hit Edele and Keavy — they could do it. Creating a band didn't have to be just a childhood dream. Their older, mega-cute brother, Shane, showed them that stardom was possible when he hit the big time with his mega-hot boy band, Boyzone. Shane's success convinced Edele and Keavy that they had to go for it — they wanted singing stardom, too.

But to make it happen, the twins needed to find two more girls with the same musical mission.

Two and Two Is Four

Enter **Sinead O'Carroll** and **Lindsay Armaou.** One day Keavy ran into fellow Irishwoman Sinead at — get this — a car garage where Keavy worked. (Yep, Keavy was an auto mechanic-in-training!) When Sinead said she needed her tire fixed, Keavy pulled on her overalls and went to work. That's when they got to talking about music. Then Sinead and Keavy settled it — they'd set up a band along with Edele. (Sinead and Edele had met in dance classes they'd taken together.) But they still needed a fourth.

Hmmm, they knew this girl named Lindsay. Lindsay took kick-boxing classes with Keavy. So it was all set — Keavy was going to talk with Lindsay. Just as they had hoped, Lindsay was way into it, and the band was born. The girls named themselves D'Zire. (Of course, that name would change later.)

"Right from the start, we hit it off musically *and* socially," Sinead explains. Getting along was a cinch because they really liked being together and talking about the future of the group. As the girls started making band plans, they discovered that each of them had different musical backgrounds — between them, they knew about everything from hip-hop to pop to soul to traditional Irish folk

tunes. "We decided to take all of our influences, absorb them, and create something that was entirely our own."

This band was gonna be so unique!

A Charming Break

Now they had a dream — to become amazing singers and, well, super-famous femmes, too. The foursome practiced like crazy and even shelled out their own dough to record their very own songs. The next goal for Sinead, Lindsay, Edele, and Keavy was to get discovered.

That's when a little luck came their way. The divas of D'Zire, as they were called then, were busy rehearsing at an Irish studio. It just so happened that a camera crew was visiting the studio to make a documentary. The crew filmed the girls, and D'Zire ended up on television. *TV!* That was their big break, because Boyzone's manager finally noticed them, and he wanted to meet them in person. Needless to say, he was completely enchanted!

The manager was so impressed that he took the girls to meet Boyzone's big-shot producer, Ray Hedges. At first Ray said no way. He thought the girls would be just like any other girl band. But when the girls sang for him, Ray's attitude did a 180. He *loooooved* them! Keavy, Edele, Lindsay, and Sinead were so different from other female acts — they were so down-to-earth and lovable. They were more like a real girl's

Laughin' out loud at the Disney Channel's Kids Awards.

best friends, not snotty superstars. Ray really liked this chick clique, but there was one little problem. Their name, D'Zire, didn't really fit the band. But since the girls had bewitched *him*, Ray suggested that they change their name to B*Witched. It was perfect. And the asterisk? "Well, that's just to be pretty," Keavy explains. "We wanted something to look a bit different on our record sleeves. But now it's taken on a life all its own!"

The Perfect Musical Brew

Their dream of having a real band was coming true, so the tunesome twins asked their brother for some rock star pointers. "He told us to be ready to work very hard," Edele said. But probably the best thing Shane did for the B*Witched chicks was asking them to open for a few of Boyzone's sold-out shows. After all, the girls still needed a record label. At one of the opening gigs, representatives from Epic, Boyzone's label, saw the girls' bubbly, bewitching performance and immediately signed them up. Finally all of their hard work was starting to pay off.

Epic decided the girls should move to London. The record label put them up in an English house early in 1997. Soon Sinead, Lindsay, Edele, and Keavy became roommates *and* best friends — singing, dancing, and writing songs all day long, getting their act in great gear.

A prime pic from Party in the Park.

Once their, as Sinead calls it, "Irish hip-hop/pop" music was perfect, they hit the road. B*Witched sang to teens and preteens at schools all over England. They did all of this before their album was released — to try to build a pack of fans. It worked! B*Witched was an instant success. Kids went coo-coo for the music, especially the song "C'est La Vie." Like magic, when the song finally got onto radio stations, it debuted at number one on the British pop charts! (That's a *trés* big deal; it hardly ever happens!)

"We didn't believe it was true — it was unreal," Edele says. "We all started crying!"

The girls are totally in sync with their raging dance grooves.

To make a long story short, their next three singles also debuted at number one on the charts in England. That's *beyond* amazing. Nobody else has had that many number ones in a row — not the Spice Girls or even the Beatles. And their singles have been huge hits in the U.S. as well!

"I still can't believe everything [that's] happened," Sinead says. She admits that she tries not to think about all of this mega-success. Instead, she and the band try to stay real — and totally down-to-earth. "We're just busy enjoying the ride at the moment," Sinead adds. "We totally believe in what we do. We totally believe in the power of pop music to raise people's spirits. And that's exactly what we intend to do — raise people's spirits and make them feel more alive."

Sinead
B★Witched

Chapter 2 Sinead O'Carroll

Gorgeous and sophisticated, Sinead's the oldest band member of B*Witched. But this twenty-one-year-old is totally used to being the first-born — she was the oldest of three kids in her family, too. Sinead was born on May 14, 1978, in Ireland, and it didn't take her long to become incredibly interested in all things musical. As a tot, she started learning how to do traditional Irish dancing. She was even a contestant in a few dance competitions when she was a preteen! Even though she was super-talented at Irish jigs, she decided to try something new. So, she started taking piano lessons and regular dance classes.

Sinead's teen life in her hometown of Kildare — which is a small town about an hour outside of Dublin — was pretty normal. She got along well with her parents, but admits that they were pretty strict. Sinead would get really jealous of her friends because they were going out and having fun. But Sinead wasn't permitted to hit the town until she turned sixteen! Oh, well, once she *did* start dating, she had a wonderful long-term boyfriend. "I went out with him for two and a half years," she says. "He'd do anything for me — and we never got into one fight!" The romance came to an end, but Sinead still has fond memories of him.

Sinead finished school and moved to Dublin, where she continued taking dance classes and worked as a nanny. Life really got exciting after she got her car fixed, of all things. That's when she met Keavy — who was helping out in her dad's garage. "We just hit it off!" Next thing she knew, she was part of a kickin' band called B*Witched!

The 411

Full name: Sinead (pronounced Shin-ade) Maria O'Carroll

Nicknames: Sin (pronounced Shin), Sin-bin, and Socky (because her initials are S O'C)

Age: 21

Birthday: May 14, 1978

Sign: Taurus

Hair: Blonde

Hometown: Kildare, Ireland

Resides: London, England

Sibs: One brother, Paul; two sisters, Elaine and Ailish

Plays: Bass guitar and piano

Speaks: English, French

Collects: Fake tattoos

Her favorites

Color: Black ("Because it's very sophisticated," she says.)

Food: Chinese

Breakfast cereal: Sugar Puffs

Ice cream: Vanilla

Toothpaste: Colgate

Perfume: Envy by Gucci

Movie: *Con Air*

Person: Mother Teresa — "I have such admiration for people who give up their lives for others."

Musician: George Michael

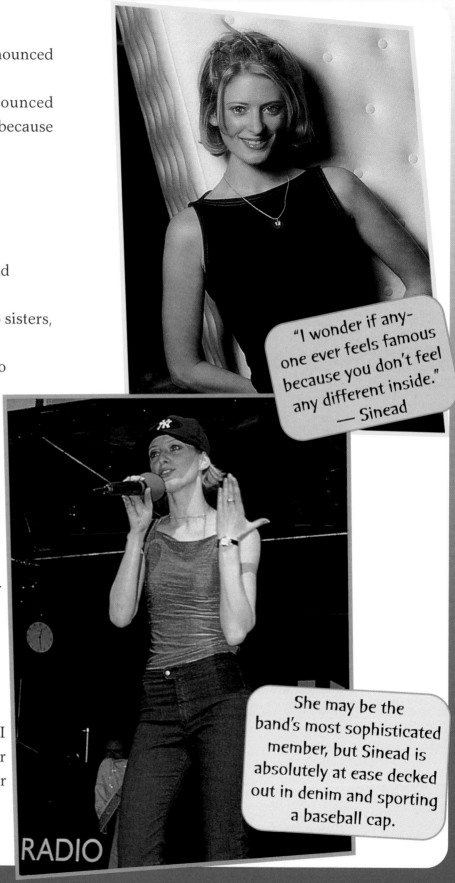

"I wonder if anyone ever feels famous because you don't feel any different inside."
— Sinead

She may be the band's most sophisticated member, but Sinead is absolutely at ease decked out in denim and sporting a baseball cap.

RADIO

More scoop on Sinead

PERSONALITY POINTS:

Describes herself: "I'm earthy, sophisticated, sensible, ambitious, and grounded."

Oops! Well, sometimes Sinead is totally forgetful. In one week, she once lost two jackets, a pair of jeans, and her B*Witched ring (each band member has one)! "She also tends to lose her false fingernails," Edele explains. "Where Sinead has been, you'll find one. It's like her trademark. And they're quite dangerous when you sit on one!"

Huh? Sometimes, Keavy says Sinead is "away with the fairies," which means she can be a bit, um, spacey. "You'll be saying to her something like, 'Pigs fly, you know,' and she'll go, 'Yeah!'" The girls kid her about it all of the time.

Sinead's a sweetie: Sinead used to work with handicapped children when she was younger.

She's smooth, too: "Sinead's so pretty that people turn around to look at her when she's out walking," Keavy says. "But she doesn't care — or even seem to notice!"

But once she was wicked . . . when she got suspended from school for launching eggs at her classmates. Naughty!

Weird habit: She brushes her teeth three or four times a day because she hates the taste of food in her mouth after she eats.

Eerie belief: Sinead believes in ghosts — but she admits she's never seen one!

Hide your stuff: She loves to borrow clothes . . . but sometimes forgets about it! "You'll ask her for your stuff, and she'll swear she put it back," Edele says. "Then ten minutes later, Sinead is always like, 'Oh, sorry, I do have it!' " Ha!

LOVE INFO:

First smooch: She was fifteen years old, and it happened on a school bus!

Boy bashful: She says she'll never approach a guy or make the first move. Why? "When I was a teenager, I was at this disco, and I asked this guy to dance because his friends told me to," she says. "So I did, and he said no! To this day I've never asked a guy to dance, and I never will."

Has she been in love before? Sinead says it happened only once. (Could it be the guy she went out with for two and a half years? Hmmm . . .) Anyway, she always refuses to dish much about her dude. . . . And sometimes she says she doesn't think she's been in love. It's difficult to know!

Lookin' for love now? "B*Witched is keeping me far too busy for a manhunt."

But one day . . . Sinead says, "My parents have been married for twenty-four years. I'd love to find someone I could be with for that long."

Sinead is all about being into her fans—so cool to have a signed CD!

RANDOM SCOOP:

Lock up your chocolate! Sinead is often known to eat like a bird when it comes to dinner. She'll leave half of her plate untouched. But when the dessert comes 'round, Sinead *always* eats a bunch. "I love chocolate cake and ice cream," she admits.

Working girl: Sinead was once an usher at a movie theater and a salesgirl in a retail shop.

Ugggh! Embarrassing moment: "Once my friends started playing spin the bottle, and each guy and girl had to stand behind this see-through glass door while everyone watched each other kiss." When the bottle landed on Sinead, she had to do the smooch. "It was so embarrassing!"

Beauty tips: "Make sure you wear foundation that matches your skin tone — you don't want a big orange ring under your chin. Also, eyelash curlers are great — they make your eyelashes look longer — buy a plastic one though, they're better than the metal ones. Finally, remember that less is more!"

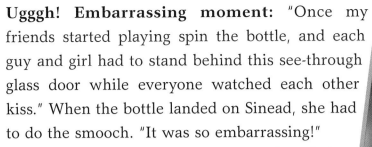

Sinead's totally okay when she's outside of the big city. "I'm a real country girl!"

"Mum and Dad have been totally supportive," Sinead says. "They had to strike out from the crowd to succeed in their businesses, so they recognize that I've had to go my own way as well."

Watch out! This cake is no match for Sinead's super sweet tooth!

Lindsay
B★Witched

Chapter 3 Lindsay Armaou

Lindsay — the bright and bubbly youngest member of B*Witched — was born in Athens, Greece, on December 12, 1980. She lived there for her first thirteen years, until her parents decided to get divorced. See, Lindsay's mom is Irish but her dad is Greek. Her mother wanted to move back to Ireland, but her dad wasn't up for that. "My dad didn't want to move his business that was in Greece," Lindsay explains. "So they decided that my dad would stay." Not only were her parents separating for good, but Lindsay was moving to a totally new country. "I didn't fully understand at first that we would be in Ireland forever. When it finally dawned on me, it was awful," she says.

Since Lindsay is an only child, she didn't have anyone to talk with about this huge change. The only time she really wished for a brother or sister was during the split, Lindsay says. "For a month or so, I could have done with someone to turn to." Lucky for Lindsay, those bad times didn't last too long. When she went off to boarding school in Dublin, things started getting much better for the normally happy teenager. "Once I made friends, everything was fine," Lindsay says. "It didn't take long until I loved Ireland — apart from missing my dad."

Meeting her future band mates made things even easier. Lindsay took dance lessons with Sinead, Edele, and Keavy. And she even took a kick-boxing class with Keavy. And when Keavy found out how musically talented Lindsay was, she snapped Linds up for the band. After all, Lindsay had been taking piano lessons since age seven, and she started playing guitar when she was thirteen. Plus, this girl's so easygoing and super-cool. That's all it took for the other three to fall for Lindsay! "We just loved her," Keavy says.

The 411

Full name: Lindsay Gael Christian Armaou
Nickname: Linds
Age: 18
Birthday: December 12, 1980
Sign: Sagittarius
Hair: Black (with blue streaks)
Hometown: Athens, Greece
Resides: London, England
Sibs: None
Plays: Piano and guitar
Speaks: Greek, English
Collects: Teddy bears
Pets: Two cats, Leah and Snoopy; and three dogs, Husky, Cheeky, and Chubby

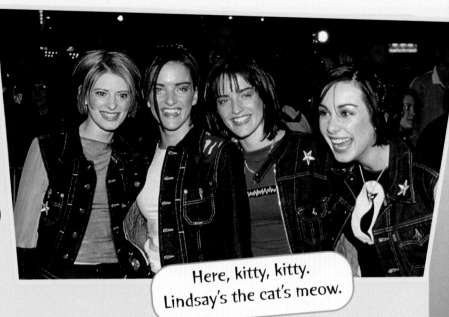

Here, kitty, kitty. Lindsay's the cat's meow.

Her favorites

Food: Bananas, mangos, and watermelon
Musicians: The Verve, All Saints, and Five
Color: Red
TV show: *Friends*
Perfume: Cool Water by Davidoff
Drink: Whole milk
Animal: Cats! Cats! Cats!

The lowdown on Lindsay

PERSONALITY POINTS:

Describes herself: "I'm ambitious, laid-back, bubbly, friendly, and sometimes even a deep girl!"
Sweet deed: When she was ten years old, she saved a litter of kittens from drowning.
Loves, loves, loves: Animals. "Lindsay can't stand anyone being nasty to critters," Sinead says.

Goes with the flow . . . Lindsay can adapt to different situations and places very easily, Sinead says.

A little gullible? Yes! "I just say some really stupid, silly joke and Lindsay will believe me," Edele explains. "Like last night, I told Lindsay that our manager said she would have to get a nose ring and an eyebrow ring. Well, Lindsay started saying, 'Oh, no!' And I was like, 'I'm only joking!' Lindsay goes, 'Oh, you *always* do that do me!'"

Cringe! Lindsay dislikes bad manners. "Politeness costs nothing, and it's horrible when people are rude."

Scares her senseless: Small spaces! "She's very claustrophobic," Edele says. "When we did our *Rollercoaster* video, we had to have safety harnesses on. Lindsay had to get out of hers a couple of times because she kept going, 'Get me out of here!'"

Makes her cry: *Titanic* — "I was literally sobbing and shaking!"

Funny habit: "Lindsay always walks around the house wearing her slippers," Sinead explains. "It drives us crazy 'cause she never lifts her feet, so they go swoosh, swoosh!"

Ever naughty? Noooooo! All the band members agree, Lindsay's a good girl.

B*Witched was in full bloom at the Top of the Pops presentations.

LOVE INFO:

First smooch: On a school bus in the sixth grade with a boy named Nico. "We dated until the summer then we hated each other!"

Love outlook: "I'm so single. I haven't had a boyfriend for absolutely yonks!"

Shared single status: "None of us have a boyfriend," Lindsay says. "And there are none on the horizon. It's a disaster! We don't get time, and even if we meet a guy for ten minutes, it can be up to four months later before we see him again."

Boys bewitch her . . . "I enjoy male company, but I like female company, too. I think girls are more on the same wavelength — boys can be a bit mysterious!"

RANDOM SCOOP:

Kickin' talent: Kick-boxing!

Sweetest gift: A fan once gave her a little statuette of a dragon that he'd painted himself. "He had put so much effort into it!"

Gets excited when . . . She speaks in Greek. Normally Lindsay will be really quiet on the phone, but when she's yapping with her father in Greek, she practically starts yelling into the phone.

Grrrr . . . Lindsay's name was spelled "Linsday" on the UK edition of the "C'est La Vie" single.

Working girl: She's been a salesgirl in a Dublin retail shop.

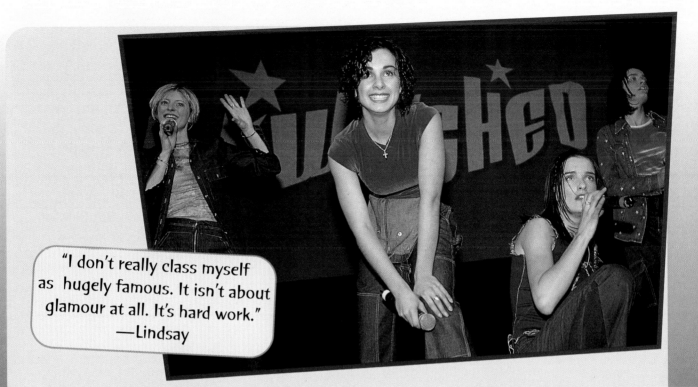

"I don't really class myself as hugely famous. It isn't about glamour at all. It's hard work."
—Lindsay

Hairy hair: Lindsay's hair used to be long and straight. It went curly when she moved to Ireland.

Highlighted hair: For two whole years, Lindsay went blonde!

Amazing talent: She's the only member of the band who can twinkle her nose like Samantha the good witch on the classic TV show *Bewitched*.

Lindsay wigged out for the ABBA tribute.

"I'm still the same with my old friends. It's important to keep in touch with them 'cuz that's where you come from and you should never forget that."

"My parents have tried hard not to let their breakup affect me, and I love them both so much!"

Edele
B★Witched

Chapter 4 Edele Lynch

Edele Lynch, the self-proclaimed leader of B*Witched, was born on December 15, 1979 (along with her twin sister, Keavy!). Her mom, Noleen, says she's not at all surprised at Edele's world-wide success. "She was always obsessed with music and writing songs," Noleen explains. But from a young age, she had another obsession as well. Edele loooooved to dance. "I studied ballet, then jazz, modern, and tap dancing," Edele says. "Then I got into hip-hop dancing." She even joined a dance troupe and toured Ireland. After all that, she even *taught* dancing for a while.

But Edele can do more than cut a rug. "She and Keavy have beautiful voices, too," their mom says. And there's more: when she was a tot, Edele would come home with writing all over the sleeves of her shirt. Her mom thought she was into poetry, but the scribbles were Edele's first attempts at songwriting. (And her mom wasn't bummed that she wrote on her shirt — she was glad Edele was into writing!)

Become *this* famous, though? Even Edele didn't dream it. She just knew she was way more into all things musical than her friends. "I remember a day when I realized I was actually *good* at it," she says. At about twelve or thirteen, she was listening to the song, "Eternal Flame" by the Bangles in the car while her mom was driving. "My mom turned around and said, 'Ah, you sing that beautifully, Edele.'" That really gave Edele the confidence she needed. And now look where she is!

The 411

Full name: Edele Claire Christina Edwina Lynch

Nickname: Eddie

Age: 19

Birthday: December 15, 1979

Sign: Sagittarius

Hair: Brown (but sometimes she dyes it red — so cute!)

Hometown: Dublin, Ireland

Resides: London, England

Sibs: One twin sister, Keavy; three sisters, Naomi, Allison, and Tara; one brother, Shane

Collects: Stuffed animals (You can't see her bed because it's piled high with teddy bears.)

Edele shows off the sweet shamrock bear she received from a fan.

Her favorites

Color: Yellow

Food: Lobster, crayfish, and shrimp

Sandwich: Chicken with loads of mayonnaise on white bread

Breakfast cereals: Cornflakes and Special K

Ice cream: Vanilla — and it absolutely has to be yellow

Drink: Milk

Perfume: Miss Dior by Christian Dior

Movie: *Clueless*

Musicians: Backstreet Boys, Cleopatra, and the Spice Girls

Childhood toy: Skateboard — "I used to ride it for hours and hours!"

People: "My mum and dad!"

More dish on Edele

PERSONALITY POINTS:

Describes herself: "I'm level-headed, stubborn, a good friend, ambitious, and a perfectionist."

Totally outgoing: "Edele likes being different and getting noticed," Lindsay says. "She likes striking colors and unusual patterns."

Watch out . . . "Usually, she's very calm and cool," Lindsay explains. "But when Edele gets angry, she gets *really* angry. Then she yells!"

Worst trait: She's sooo stubborn. "And it drives everyone mad!" Edele says.

Mischievous girl: "When I was in school, if it was raining and we arrived wet, we were allowed to go home and change," Edele explains. "So every time it rained, I made sure that I didn't take my umbrella with me, and I would stand in the rain a little bit longer so I got soaked through. If I ever arrived dry, I'd go to the bathroom and throw water all over myself. Either way, I'd get sent home. It was grand!"

Can't take: Spiders or roller coasters — ironic!

Scares her to death . . . A dark room! Edele always carries a night-light with her when she travels.

Edele shines on stage.

First kisses: "He was my brother's friend, Christopher, and I met him BMX-ing [BMX is a kind of off-road bike]. Oh, then there was this boy named Patrick. He was the only boy in my metalwork class who would talk to me 'cause I was the only girl!"

Lost love: After going out with her then-boyfriend for eighteen months, Edele had to break up with him. "B*Witched went to England, and I never saw him," she says about their attempt at a long-distance romance. "It just wasn't fair to us to try to have a relationship." Awwww!

Forever friends, though . . . "When I'm back home, I still see him but it's just as friends now."

RANDOM SCOOP:

She's sooo superstitious . . . Edele always has to take the third microphone whenever she's onstage. Plus, before she goes onstage, she has to

Edele gets fired up in her flaming denim dungarees.

bless herself. "She always makes me bless myself after her, so I do," Keavy says. "But then two seconds before we go on, she'll bless herself again and insist that I do it again, too!"

Working girl: She used to be a salesgirl at a shop called Stadium Sports.

Ouch! You know the scar between Edele's eyebrows? She got that while spinning 'round and 'round on her second birthday. She fell right into their concrete fireplace and ended up with eighteen stitches! Ugggh!

Another ouch! Edele used to do gymnastics but hurt her knee really badly when she was thirteen. She had to give it up.

First shot at fame . . . She was on a TV show called *Joe Maxi.* The show hosts visited her school and taught them all how to do handstands. Guess Edele did a great one!

Poor Lindsay: Edele hates cats!

You'd never guess: She has a hidden talent for jewelry making. "I once made an arm bracelet out of a fork!"

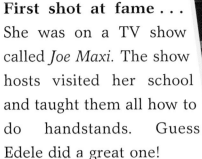

"We're not a girl band, we're a tomboy band!"

"People always think twins have a special intuition. I think it's true. I can tell if Keavy's upset. If she's gone, I'll get a sudden feeling when something's wrong with her."

When Edele once said, "I'm probably a little stubborn," the others replied, "a little?"

These four girls are here to stay!

Keavy
B★Witched

Chapter 5 Keavy Lynch

Keavy is actually twenty minutes older than her twin sister, Edele. They were both born on December 15, 1979, but at least Keavy can claim a slight age advantage!

Ever since Keavy was tiny, she has shared her sister's love for dancing and singing. "If I ever had any worries, I would start performing," Keavy says. "I'd dance my troubles away!" Her whole family pretty much did the same thing. There were six kids, and they were always putting on little shows. Keavy was way into it! She was a natural.

But she also had another talent: She really liked fixing cars. Between her schoolwork, dance classes, and kick-boxing lessons, Keavy took on a part-time job. "I started working in my dad's garage when I was seventeen," she says. "People would ask, 'Where's the tire guy?' and I would tell them, 'You're looking at him.' " Another duty for this mechanic-in-training was to check people's oil. "It was just a job, but I really loved it."

Still, Keavy was quick to leave her grease monkey career behind when the band got together. Thank goodness for Keavy, though. What would have happened if Keavy hadn't been at the garage when Sinead wandered in needing her tire fixed? And Keavy was the one who had kick-boxing class with Lindsay, so she's the one who really reeled Linds in. And well, of course, she's Edele's twin sister. Talk about the glue that binds B*Witched together — it's the band's shyest member — Keavy!

The 411

Full name: Keavy-Jane Elizabeth Annie Lynch
Nickname: Keaves
Age: 19
Birthday: December 15, 1979
Sign: Sagittarius
Hair: Brown ("But I have some purple bits in it to make it look more colorful!")
Hometown: Dublin, Ireland
Resides: London, England
Sibs: One twin sister, Edele; three sisters, Naomi, Allison, and Tara; one brother, Shane
Plays: Saxophone, drums, and guitar
Tattoo: A Japanese symbol on her left shoulder that means happiness.

Keavy is the key— she helped bring B*Witched together!

Her favorites

Color: Purple
Food: Chicken
Perfume: Dune by Christian Dior
Music: Savage Garden, Janet Jackson, and Boyzone
Movie: *Sleepless in Seattle*
Her car: Volkswagen Golf GTI. "I fix the tires and stuff myself!"

Keavy tidbits

PERSONALITY POINTS:
Describes herself: "I'm a shy, laid-back, cute, giddy, and happy girl!"

She doesn't look like much of a tomboy now.

Her sister says Keavy's . . . "Too quiet for her own good. Sometimes she doesn't say much."

Funny habit: Keavy freaks if she has to sit on the right side of the seat. She always has to sit on the left. Same thing with sleeping, Keavy always sleeps on the left side of the bed.

Amazing talent: She's known for talking in a high voice like a chipmunk.

Sooo sensitive: Keavy admits she's super-emotional. For instance, she missed her mom's birthday last year and nearly cried!

Maybe she'd change . . . How embarrassed she gets. "All the time, I get so embarrassed. I hate it!"

All laughs: "Sometimes when I'm nervous, I can't help laughing," Keavy says. "Like if I'm at the doctor's or somewhere I start to giggle. Then when everyone starts staring at me, I'll go, 'Oops! Sorry, I'm just nervous.' "

Oops! "One day I was messing around, and I managed to break the window in my bedroom," Keavy says. "I kept quiet and hoped no one would notice." Well, that night there was a rainstorm. "When everyone woke up, they thought lightning had broken it. They felt sorry for me and thought I must've been terrified." Now Keavy feels bad that she never 'fessed up. "Mum and Dad, I'm sorry!"

Hey, Keavy—caught you looking.

LOVE INFO:

First smooch: "I was about twelve, and it was with a guy called Dax who's Shane's friend from Portugal. I remember being very nervous."

Bye-bye boyfriend: She split up with her boyfriend on New Year's Eve.

Still flirty: "I see all of these cute boys but I only get to talk to them for about ten minutes, then it's time to get back on the tour bus. We all enjoy flirting, and that's the tragedy of it!"

Lifelong love: "If I find the love of my life, I wouldn't care if he was the milkman, the paperboy, or what he did."

RANDOM SCOOP:

Aspiring model: When Keavy was little, she appeared on a holiday camp calendar.

Yakkety-yak: "Keavy's on the phone from seven P.M. until midnight," says Edele. "And the next day people say, 'I was trying to call you all night!' Keavy's phone bills are huuuuuge!"

Skidding out: Sometimes Keavy missteps on stage. "Keavy stepped on the back of Edele's shoe three different times, and each time it came clean off," Lindsay says. "The last time, Edele had to finish the performance with just one shoe. Afterward, everyone was asking what happened!"

Whoops! Keavy's name tag is misspelled. So unfair!

One wish: "I'd like to have smaller feet! They're size five, but if they were size four, I could share shoes with my sister!"

Keavy pierced? Yep. She had a tongue piercing, but she took it out. "I had to eat soup for ages," she says.

Beauty tip: "Get plenty of sleep — we don't do that sometimes," Keavy says. "It's good to eat well, too."

Hates, hates, hates: Smoking. "Urgh! Disgusting!"

Never without: Her starry yellow pillow that a fan gave her. She plops it down wherever she goes.

Keavy's motto: "Live life to the fullest and work really hard!"

"For us, it's just about making music. That's what makes us happy."

"Sometimes our fans know where we're scheduled to be before we do! They'll say you're here next week, and we're like, 'We are?' We can't keep track of all the places we go!"

"Somebody once told me that I had the most gorgeous smile. That's lovely because it's important to smile!"

Chapter 6 Wow! What a Famous Family!

If you live in Dublin, Ireland, and your last name is Lynch, you're practically destined to be a star. Just look at Keavy and Edele! And, of course, there's Shane—their very famous Boyzone big brother. But every member of this multitalented family has an interesting story!

First of all, Noleen and Brendan, the mom and dad of the house, were way into music even when *they* were growing up. Brendan's dad played the fiddle, and he taught Brendan to play, too. He even taught the instrument to a famous Irish folk band called the Dubliners. So when Noleen and Brendan had their own family, it was only natural to introduce them to music. All six of the Lynch children grew up dancing and singing together. To them, performing just meant playtime. But they all dreamed of stardom.

So what about Shane?

Shane was the one who reached the big time first. When he was seventeen, he helped form the band Boyzone. They soared to success in Ireland and England, much like 'N Sync and the Backstreet Boys did in Europe before making it in the United States. So did Shane's success spur Edele and Keavy to follow in his footsteps? "Well, we were always saying that we were going to be in a band together — myself and Keavy," Edele says. "But the thing with Shane and Boyzone is that they opened up the commercial market in Ireland itself."

See, before Boyzone, there weren't that many pop bands who hailed from Ireland. So Shane really helped the girls in that way; in fact Boyzone made it easier for all aspiring Irish pop bands. Plus, Shane was able to get B*Witched a few gigs when they were just starting out. That was a huge help, too.

So are the twins and Shane super-close? Oh, yes! When Shane left home to tour with Boyzone, the girls missed him

The boys of Boyzone: Shane is in the middle.

something awful. But when they started getting their music together, Shane called all the time with pointers. Maybe a few too many pointers — B*Witched eventually knocked Boyzone right off the top of the pop charts in England with their debut song, "C'est La Vie"! While "C'est La Vie" was number one on the British chart, Boyzone's CD, *Where We Belong,* was the number-one album! What good fortune!

What was it like to compete though? It was great because the sibs weren't really competing at all. They were all just super-happy for each other. "Shane was so excited about Edele and Keavy's success with their band," Noleen says. "He was more excited about their success than any of his own success with Boyzone." Plus, like Edele and Keavy said, it was great that someone knew what they were going through when they first hit the big time. "He told us our feet wouldn't touch the ground for a while," Edele says. "He was right!"

And the other super-cool siblings?

The talent doesn't stop with those stories of stardom. All the sibs are successful. Their oldest sister is an engineer in the U.S. The twins' youngest sister, Naomi, was second in the European Dancing Championship in May 1998. Tara, another sister, is starting her own band called TAB! "They're great!" Edele attests. So watch for them on the charts next!

Despite all of the action in the Lynch family, Noleen insists that they're very normal. "We're ordinary, and they're ordinary teenagers," she says. Noleen says all she did was encourage them to follow their dreams and to work hard. Maybe the one way the Lynches are different from most families is that they hardly ever get to see each other. . . . With everyone's schedule, rarely are they home at the same time. But when they are, they don't talk music. They just catch up on each other's personal lives.

Totally twins.

They miss their parents, too!

Still, Edele and Keavy get lonely for their totally sweet family. Edele says Shane warned them that that might happen. "And they *are* lonely; they call home every day!" Noleen says.

Chapter 7 An Enchanting Q 'n' A

Here's the scoop on your most-asked, most-compelling questions. Check out how the band has responded in the past to your favorite inquiries. It's a quest fest!

1. Does B*Witched get along with the Spice Girls?

"Yes! We totally respect the Spice Girls!" Edele says. "We have performed with them — it proves that we are all great friends and are happy to help each other out."

2. Does B*Witched get bummed when people compare them to the Spice Girls?

"You're always going to be compared to someone because you're new, and nobody knows how to describe you yet," Keavy explains. "Still, I think to be compared to the Spice Girls is cool because they've been so successful.

They opened the door for girl bands. They showed everybody that girls can do it, too!"

3. Did the girls in B*Witched *really* come together on their own, or were they brought together by a record company?

"Noooo! We've been together for more than two years!" Sinead explains. "We all knew each other from dance classes. Then I met up with Keavy when I got my car fixed at a garage where she worked. Keavy found Lindsay because they took kick-boxing class together. We formed the band all on our own!"

The girls go glam in their seventies chic for the ABBA tribute.

4. We've heard rumors that Sinead isn't really twenty-one — that she's more like twenty-six — is that true? What does Sinead say?

"No, I'm not twenty-six, I'm twenty-one," Sinead says. "People are always going to say things like that. It doesn't bother me."

(Note: According to the newspaper *The Sunday Mirror*, a high school classmate of Sinead's came forward on the age issue. She said, "I'm twenty-six now and Sinead was in my class so I can't work out how she's only twenty-one!" *Oh, well, no matter how old she is, Sinead's still super-cool in our book!*)

5. Okay, time for a fun question. Now that B*Witched is so busy, do they ever have time to, well, have fun?

"Well, when we were in Germany, we couldn't resist having a snowball fight! We were on our way home from performing and saw the snow," Keavy says. "Of course, we had to get the car to stop, so we could jump out and have a desperate snowball fight. By the time we got to our hotel, we were soaked!"

6. What song did B*Witched do for the ABBA tribute concert?

"We did a tribute of ABBA's single 'Thank You for the Music,'" Edele says. "We did the song with Steps and Billie. We loved doing it because even though we don't remember [ABBA], we know they were massive."

These lasses have the luck (and laughter) of the Irish.

7. How do the B*Witched chicks feel about being so famous now?

"It's weird," Sinead says. "But we don't really feel famous. Like when we first watched ourselves performing 'C'est La Vie' on a television show, we couldn't believe it was actually us. It was like our absolute dream come true!"

8. How long will B*Witched stay together?

Keavy says she spoke to Celine Dion about this subject once. "She told us that the important thing to do is keep the band together and stay friends," Keavy explains. "That will be easy! We hope we're together forever!"

Chapter 8 B*Witching Quiz
Every girl in this band is wicked cool -

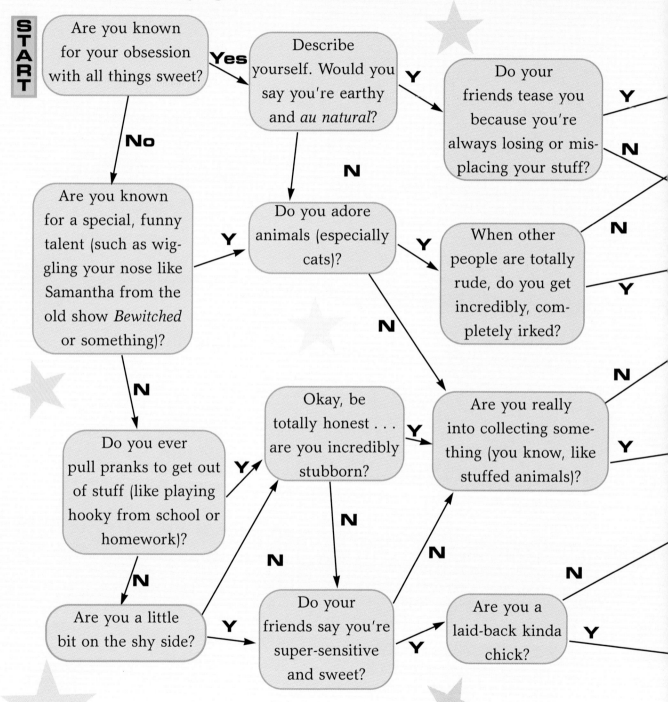

START

Are you known for your obsession with all things sweet?

Yes → Describe yourself. Would you say you're earthy and *au natural*?

No → Are you known for a special, funny talent (such as wiggling your nose like Samantha from the old show *Bewitched* or something)?

Y → Do your friends tease you because you're always losing or misplacing your stuff?

N → Do you adore animals (especially cats)?

Y → When other people are totally rude, do you get incredibly, completely irked?

N → Are you really into collecting something (you know, like stuffed animals)?

Do you ever pull pranks to get out of stuff (like playing hooky from school or homework)?

Y → Okay, be totally honest . . . are you incredibly stubborn?

N → Are you a little bit on the shy side?

Y → Do your friends say you're super-sensitive and sweet?

Y → Are you a laid-back kinda chick?

– but which girl is the most like *you*?

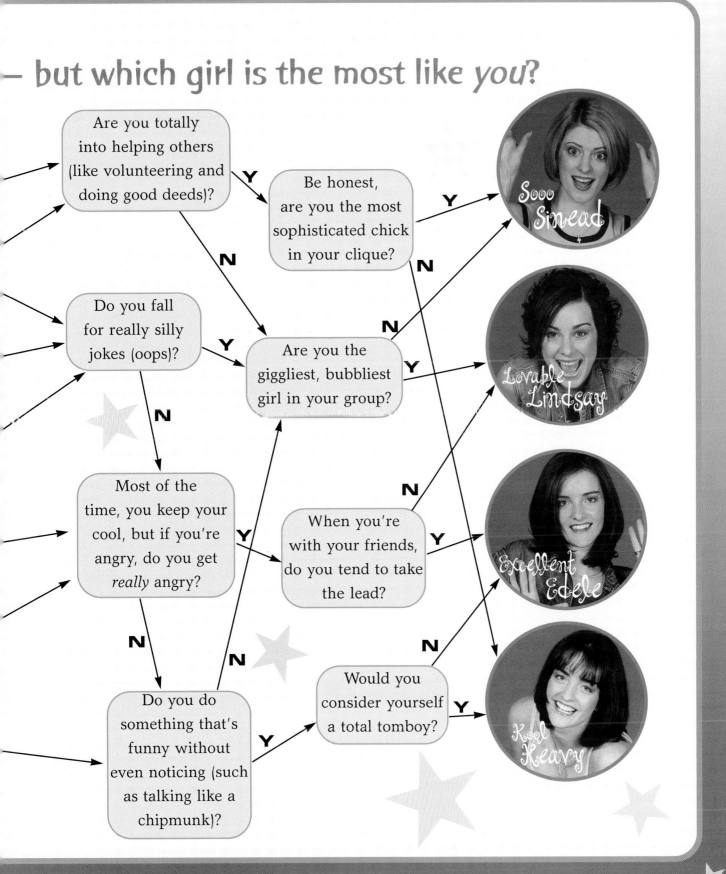

Are you totally into helping others (like volunteering and doing good deeds)?

Y → Be honest, are you the most sophisticated chick in your clique?

Y → Sooo Sinead

N

Do you fall for really silly jokes (oops)?

Y → Are you the giggliest, bubbliest girl in your group?

N

N

N

Y → Lovable Lindsay

Most of the time, you keep your cool, but if you're angry, do you get *really* angry?

Y → When you're with your friends, do you tend to take the lead?

Y → Excellent Edele

N

N

N

Do you do something that's funny without even noticing (such as talking like a chipmunk)?

Y → Would you consider yourself a total tomboy?

Y → Kool Keavy

N

Which B*Witched chick would you be?

Excellent Edele
You're probably headstrong and *super*-sure of your *super*-cool self. So it's totally expected that you'd take the lead when it comes to your buds — that's also what Edele does! You're probably very passionate — that's why you're into collecting, something you totally love. But, wait a second, sister. . . . No one had better be messin' with you. You're likely to tell people how it is when you get peeved. But you don't stay mad long — you'd rather laugh and have lots of fun!

Sooo Sinead
Just like the oldest member of B*Witched, you're the perfect mix of hippy chick and totally chic. Sinead loves to wear black because it makes her feel sophisticated — we wouldn't be surprised to learn that you do the same thing. Anyway, you like to stay down-to-earth, and are super-caring and conscientious, too. But whoa, baby! Nothing comes between you and dessert. Maybe that's because you're so super-sweet.

Kool Keavy
No one would call you the loudest of the bunch. That's because you prefer to be low-key, and yeah, well, you're kinda quiet, too. You keep to yourself, except when you're with your girls, then you let it all hang out. But you're totally not afraid to be unique—and your inner tomboy comes out sometimes. Another personality plus? Your pals probably turn to you when they need to talk. They know you're always sensitive and completely cool!

Lovable Lindsay
Does anything ever get you down? If it does, just like Lindsay, you bounce back fast. That's because you've got a great, totally positive 'tude about life. You smile all of the time and laugh more — even when someone's lightheartedly teasing you. As nice as you are, it's no surprise that you probably have a huge soft spot for all critters with fur. And cats! There's a good chance you loooove them. You probably have a ton of friends, too. Why? You're the purr-fect pal!

You know, you could have a lot of qualities in common with all the B*Witched chicks. This quiz just hits on a few of the girls' different traits. The truth is, no matter which girl the quiz matches you with, you'll always be totally you — and that's totally cool.

The talk of the Irish

Yes, the gabby girls of B*Witched speak English, but sometimes their words are a little different, because they have picked up some special slang. Here's a guide to the funny things they say and words you may not have heard before.

VOCAB WORDS:

to be "away with the fairies" To be ditzy or spacey.

"blokes" Another word for guys or boys.

"bezzy chum" Best friend!

"gobsmacked" To be completely in awe of something.

"knickies" A funny word for underwear.

"nosh" Another word for kissing (as in, "They noshed.").

"peckish" This means hungry.

"pressie" Another word for present.

"snog" A kiss.

"stuff up" This means mess up (as in, "That girl stuffed up!").

"wind her up" When you tease somebody (as in, "Edele really winds Lindsay up.").

Chapter 9 Kickin' Concerts

B*Witched's music is always kickin', but in concert it's totally rockin'. Getting to see them live is the coolest. The whole audience gets into it, and you can feel the music go through you. When you watch B*Witched, you can tell how much they love performing. You can also tell that they are truly awesome girls who would make amazingly fun friends.

Let the Fun Begin

When they're on stage, the fab femmes of B*Witched are all about having fun. They look their hippest, all decked out in denim. And they just can't stop smiling — maybe it's because they are all fulfilling their dreams. Edele, Keavy, Lindsay, and Sinead love sharing their music with all their fans. In their official British bio, Sinead said if B*Witched's music "brings a smile to your face, then that makes us very, very happy."

Step by Step

Be warned: At the very beginning of a concert, B*Witched comes out dancing, and they just don't stop. They've got tons of sweet moves, and they are *so* in sync with their hip-hoppin' dance steps. It's obvious they've been practicing together for a long time, not to mention the eons of dance classes they took even before B*Witched was born.

These girls can groove. They're all super-peppy and the crowd goes crazy singing and dancing along.

The In Crowd

B*Witched has toured with some of the hottest groups around. They opened for 98° on the sold-out Heat It Up tour, and they joined 'N Sync for part of the boys' first full-tilt U.S. tour. Lucky girls! And, of course, they worked with Boyzone in the very beginning (Thanks Shane!). For the ABBA tribute, B*Witched performed with Billie, the British teenage pop diva, and Steps. Keavy, Sinead, Lindsay, and Edele are all in good company!

In addition to traditional touring, B*Witched has also appeared at malls and in schools to promote their new singles. One of the best benefits of band life? They've hit some amazing spots: from Japan to Australia to Italy to Sweden. They get around!

Rev It Up

They're so hip, so talented, and well, so bewitching. If you're a real fan, you've gotta see them live. And remember, they feel super-proud when their fans go mad for them in the audience. What a massive thrill!

Chapter 10 Spellbinding Stuff

Betcha Never Heard These Fun Facts About B*Witched!

Just when you thought you knew *everything* about the band, here's more important info.

1. Once upon a time, this enchanting band called themselves Sister instead of B*Witched! In their British bio, they also say they went by Sassy until they found out another band had that name.

2. Lindsay's eyes change colors — "from green to orange to brown."

3. If Keavy could magically morph into anyone on earth for a day, she'd choose to look like Edele! "Then I'd know what it's like looking at me," she says.

4. Think a French song title is a little strange for a totally Irish band? "We *had* to put some French in there," Keavy jokes. "Just to show our teachers we learned something." In French, *c'est la vie* means *that's life.*

5. The B*Witched girls helped write nine out of the twelve songs on their debut album. *Impr*ssive!*

6. B*Witched got to play for Prince William — who enthusiastically sang along to their songs. And the girls swear they didn't even get nervous.

7. But Sinead did get really embarrassed once. She finished an interview and then realized that one of her fake nails was dangling from her hair! Ugggh . . .

8. Lindsay turned down the chance to study at a business college because she wanted to be in B*Witched so badly. And that was waaaay before they got famous.

9. When Keavy was little, she wanted to be a firewoman!

10. The night they heard that they went to number one with "C'est La Vie," they went to Planet Hollywood. They didn't party for long, though. They were still in bed by 10:30 that night!

11. What's the band's favorite drink? They're into milk!

12. They may be successful, but they still wash their own denim duds. "Sometimes, if we're in a rush to leave the house, and our clothes aren't dry, we have to wear them as they are," Keavy says. "And damp denim isn't comfortable, I can tell ya!"

13. Also, the girls have been known to dye their own hair in hotel rooms. What a colorful way to spend an evening.

14. Rumor has it that each girl owns at least fifteen pairs of jeans. (How'd ya like to raid their closets?!)

15. B*Witched is the youngest girl group ever to have a number-one hit!

The Ultimate Song Chart

Here's the lyrical lowdown of all the tunes on B*Witched's album, *B*Witched*. As Edele explains: "All of our songs are based on our own experiences." Read on for more info . . .

Let's Go (The B*Witched Jig)

This song is meant for dancin'. Onstage, the girls have a mini shake-your-booty competition. Lindsay and Sinead do Irish dancing; Edele and Keavy do a streetwise jig.

C'est La Vie

It's a modern fairy tale about being young and making the most of it. "That's pretty much how we feel right now!" Edele says.

Rev It Up

Talk about excited and happy! That's the meaning of this tune. "It's a really summery song, too," Edele adds.

To You I Belong

Keavy and Edele wrote this one for their parents. So sweet!

Rollercoaster

Of course, sometimes life is full of its ups and downs. But this song is mostly about the fun times.

Blame It on the Weatherman

One of the girls — Sinead, Lindsay, Edele, or Keavy — has some memories of a past relationship . . . and this tune is about it. But no one has revealed which girl the song is talking about!

We Four Girls

Well, you guessed it! This one's self-explanatory . . .

Castles in the Air

"It might sound like a soppy love song, but it's actually how we felt about being number one. Amazing!" Edele explains.

Freak Out

When you hear this song, simply get up and dance to it — that's the point, Edele says.

Like the Rose

Yep, it's about love. "But not just with a boyfriend, also with your family and friends," Edele adds.

Never Giving Up

Again, this one has a title that sums it up!

Oh Mr. Postman

Ever lost touch with someone you care about? Then this tune's for you.

Chapter 11 Wanna Get With B*Witched?

Write or E-mail them at the addresses below. And check the following Web sites for up-to-the-minute info!

E-mail address:

b-witched@b-witched.com

Send them snail mail in England:

(Don't forget to pay for extra postage since you're sending mail out of the United States!)

**B*Witched
c/o Trinity Street
FREEPOST
3 Alveston Place
Leamington Spa
CV32 4BR**

Web sites:

1. Official Epic site:

http://www.epicrecords.com /EpicCenter/custom/1063/

At this site, you can register to receive the absolute latest B*Witched information via E-mail. Keep up with all of their TV appearances and concert dates. (And see some live video clips, too!)

2. Official European B*Witched site:

http://www.b-witched.com

This Web site has absolutely everything you need to know. Read the latest interviews with the band, or send your friends a B*Witched postcard or post a B*Witched-specific message or story for other fans to read!

> "Our fans are quite nice. There's even a group in England that always meets us at the airport and gives us travel sweets for when we go on long journeys."
> — Sinead

> "E-mail us! We'd love to hear from you!"
> — B*Witched

Join the B*Witched Fan Club:

Mail a postcard with your name, age, street address, and E-mail address to the following address:

**B*Witched Fan Club
c/o Bravado International Group
150 South Rodeo Drive
Suite 130
Beverly Hills, CA 90212**

To follow up you can call 310-777-6580, but first get an adult's permission because this number is probably long distance.

Chapter 12 The B*Witched Crystal Ball
Know everything about the band's future plans!

A new album!

That's right! The girls were in the middle of recording their second CD in April 1999. They had a blast! If all goes well, it will be released by the end of 1999.

Here's what Keavy says: "Everything about it is top secret! But our next single will be off the new album."

Tour dates

Yay! You've gotta see B*Witched live. They rock! Here's where to find the B*Witched girls' concert schedule. Check www.epicrecords.com/EpicCenter/custom/1063 for the latest listings.

Where the girls have already been:

Well, they've been all over the world, even to Japan! They've also hit the U.S.!

B*Witched opened for 'N Sync, Britney Spears, and 98° all across the country in 1999. They also got to be on *The Rosie O'Donnell Show*, *Ricki Lake*, *Donny and Marie*, *Regis and Kathie Lee*, and a Disney special. Keep a watch out for upcoming events, too!

"We totally believe in the power of pop music to raise people's spirits. That's exactly what we intend to do. If our music can make people feel more alive, we're achieving our ambition."
— Keavy

"We're exactly the same as when we first met. Honest! If one of us did start getting affected [by all of this fame], we'd bring them straight back down."
— Sinead

I'M SPELLBOUND

4. EVER

YOU'RE B*WITCHING

I LOVE YOU

What a B*Witchingly sweet band!